Petula, Who Wouldn't Take A Bath

by Linda Bailey • art by Jackie Snider

HarperCollinsPublishersLtd

An Alligator Press Book
Consulting Editor, Dennis Lee

Published by
HarperCollins Publishers Ltd
Suite 2900, Hazelton Lanes
55 Avenue Road
Toronto, Canada M5R 3L2

96 97 98 99   First Edition   5 4 3 2 1

Canadian Cataloguing in Publication Data
Bailey, Linda, 1948-
Petula, who wouldn't take a bath
ISBN 0-00-223903-5 (bound)
ISBN 0-00-648088-8 (pbk.)
I. Snider, Jackie. II. Title.
PS8553.A55P48 1996   jC813'.54   C95-931806-2
PZ7.B35Pe 1996

With thanks, to the wonderful women in my writers' group:
Jennifer Catchpole, Ellen McGinn, Gina McMurchy-Barber,
Jennifer Mitton, Pauline Rankin and Nona Saunders.

L.B.

For Mum and Dad,
and in memory of Mister.

J.S.

Now you may not believe this (I swear that it's true):
A girl named Petula had so much to do,
she couldn't find time to get certain things done,
like naptime and clean-up — the things that aren't fun.
Especially she couldn't find time for a bath.
When her mother said "Bath time!" Petula just laughed
and ran off to get even dirtier still.
Her name was Petula Priscilla McDill.

One night after dinner, her mother called out,
"Pe-tooooo-la!
Pe-tooooo-la!
Time to take a bath now, dear.
Time to take a bath."

"Oh, NO!" cried Petula. "It's time now to play.
Amy and Jamie are coming this way.
And we're going to hunt for the two-headed snake
we saw from the tree house that Dad helped me make.
It had shiny green skin. It had huge fiery eyes.
It had jaws that could open as wide as the skies.
And we're going to catch it. Just see if we don't.
So I can't take a bath now. I can't and I won't!"

"Petula," her mom said. "Get into the tub."
"Petula," her mom said. "You need a good scrub.
If you don't very soon get some bath water flowing,
you'll be dirty enough to start vegetables growing."

Well, did that scare Petula? No! Not for a minute.
Wherever the fun was, Petula was in it.
But the funny thing was that the very next morning,
she woke up to find (there was really no warning),
that all of a sudden she couldn't quite hear,
which should not be surprising because from her ear
grew a carrot!
Yes! A carrot!

Now a carrot would be quite distressing to me
if it grew from my ear for the whole world to see.
But Petula, who felt she had nothing to hide,
tied a bow 'round the carrot and hurried outside.
And she laughed.

Later that morning, her mom called again:
"Pe-tooooo-la!
Pe-tooooo-la!
Time to take a bath now, dear.
Time to take a bath."
"Oh, NO!" cried Petula. "It's time to explore.
I just found an earthworm, and maybe there's more.
And there's brown yucky stuff dripping out of this tree,
and it sticks to your finger. Why don't you come see?
Here's a log that looks just like a huge alligator.
It's perfect for riding. I'll take a bath later."

Well now, that's what she said. But that's not what she did.
When her mom called her later, she ran off and hid
in the dog house, which certainly wasn't too clever.
(A dog house can make a girl dirtier than ever.)
So she went to bed filthy and woke up the same,
and I know you'll agree she had no one to blame
but herself (for her poor mom had tried, heaven knows).
And now the green plants sprouting up from her toes
were potatoes!
Yes! Potatoes!

Now, wouldn't you feel just a little bit silly
if potatoes grew out of your toes willy-nilly?
But Petula was different. She calmly began
to water those sprouts with her watering can.
And she laughed.

Her mom sounded tired as she called out that day:
"Pe-tooooo-la!
Pe-tooooo-la!
Time to take a bath now, dear.
Time to take a bath."

"Oh, NO!" cried Petula. "It's time now to dance.
I'm wearing my silver and green dancing pants.
I can float like a cloud. I'm as light as the air.
When I jump over here, I land way over there.
I can hang upside-down by my toes from this tree.
So I just don't have time for a bath.
Can't you see?"

Well, her mom couldn't see. But then, what could she do?
Her little girl wouldn't touch soap or shampoo.
So the very next morning, on opening her eyes,
Petula was in for a nasty surprise.
Now you may think it's mean. You might think it's unfair.
But I just have to tell you that out of her hair
grew tomatoes!
Yes! Tomatoes!

Don't you think it would give you a bit of a scare
to see green tomatoes spring out of your hair?
But Petula was quite an adventurous type.
All she said was, "I wonder when they will be ripe."
And she laughed.

To Petula, the whole thing was just a big joke.
She continued to laugh as a huge artichoke,
seven onions, two turnips and ten rows of peas
grew up over her face and crept down past her knees,
until finally Petula was all over green:
the most fantastic garden that you've ever seen.
Yes! A garden!

Well, there's nothing like going a little bit seedy
to make all your neighbors get grabby and greedy.
Have you noticed how people who see too much food
can forget what they've learned and get terribly rude?
The neighbors were shoving. They started to bicker.
The problem was everyone wanted to pick her!

They grabbed at her hair. They yanked at her toes.
They twirled her around and they nibbled her nose.
The littlest neighbor was chewing her ear
when she leaped up and yelled for the whole mob to hear:
"This isn't funny!"
And she didn't laugh.

From out of the crowd came a weak little sound
where her mother lay trampled out flat on the ground:
"Pe-tooooo-la?
Pe-tooooo-la?
Time to take a bath NOW, dear?
Time to take a bath NOW?"

"Oh, YES!" cried Petula. She ran in the door.
"Why didn't you call me for bath time before?"

She threw in the soap. She turned on the water.
She poured in some bubbles her mother had bought her,
and cheerfully, blissfully leaped in the tub.
She squealed with delight as she started to scrub.

Oh, she spluttered and gurgled. She rolled and she thrashed.
She swam and she dived and she splattered and splashed.
The bubbles flew up to the ceiling and walls,
and the water splashed over and flowed down the halls.
The most beautiful bath time that you've ever seen,
and after it ended,
Petula
      was
           clean.

And she smiled. Mmmmmmmmmmm.

So now, even if bath time is something you hate,
you should know it's the one thing that really can't wait.
The next time *your* mom says you need a good scrub,
please remember Petula and . . .